W9-CCN-190

This book is dedicated to
my brother
Michael J. San Souci

with thanks for his love, support, and boundless enthusiasm which has been both a source of inspiration and has added immeasurably to the satisfaction of writing and publishing.

This is also to acknowledge my debt to him for use of some of his original research and writing on John Henry, which helped give the present collection a starting point and a focus—and gave me the determination to do justice (I use this word advisedly, Mike!) to the more-than-life-sized men and women whose stories follow.
—R.S.S.

To my new nephews, Adam and Linden,
e alla mia nuova nipotina, Chiara.
—A.G.

Published by Doubleday,
a division of Bantam Doubleday Dell Publishing Group, Inc.
666 Fifth Avenue, New York, New York   10103

Doubleday
and the portrayal of an anchor with a dolphin are trademarks of Doubleday,
a division of Bantam Doubleday Dell Publishing Group, Inc.

Designed by Richard Oriolo

Library of Congress Cataloging-in-Publication Data
San Souci, Robert D.

Larger than life: the adventures of American legendary heroes/by Robert D. San Souci; illustrated by
Andrew Glass.
     p.   cm.
Summary: A collection of five short tales about such
legendary American heroes as John Henry, Old Storm-
along, Slue-Foot Sue, and Paul Bunyan.
     1. Tales—United States.   2. Tall tales—United States.
[1. Tall tales.   2. Folklore—United States.]   I. Glass,
Andrew, ill.   II. Title.   89-35692
PZ8.1.S227Lar   1991   CIP
398.22′0973—dc20   AC
ISBN 0-385-24907-1
RL: 3.7
Copyright © 1991 by Robert D. San Souci
Illustrations copyright © 1991 by Andrew Glass

Contents

John Henry: The Steel-Driving Man

Folks still talk about the night John Henry was born. Lightning flashed, and the whole of Virginia shook like there was an earthquake. These events marked the birth of an extraordinary baby to good Preacher Henry and his wife. Some folks say John weighed forty-four pounds the night he was born.

Even as a baby, John loved hammering things. By the time he was ten, he could hammer down fence posts as well as a grown man.

By the age of eighteen, he was over six feet tall, weighed more than two hundred and fifty pounds, and was as strong as a locomotive, with muscles like steel. He could lift two cows with two hands, or toss a hundred-pound anvil with one.

Often, while he was working on his parents' small farm, he would listen to the far-off sound of the train whistle. It was like music to his ears and seemed to be calling him.

In the evening, while the family sat on the porch, he would say, "I'm gonna be a steel driver for the railroad someday. I'm gonna be the *best* steel driver in the whole of Virginia. Maybe the whole United States."

One day a man called Little Bill stopped by Preacher Henry's for a drink of water. While he drank, he and John Henry got to talking.

"Someday, I'll drive steel for the railroad," said John.

Bill said, "I'm gonna go work for the railroad, too. They're digging tunnels through the mountains, and they need good men. Why don't you hire on with me?"

John Henry's mind was made up before the other man stopped talking.

When his mother tried to talk him out of it, Preacher Henry said, "A man ain't nothin' but a man. There's a job for him to do, and we can't stand in his way."

So John Henry set out with Little Bill.

They went together to West Virginia. There the friends signed on with the Chesapeake & Ohio—called the C&O—railroad crew, working on the Big Bend Tunnel. At one and a quarter miles, this would be the longest railroad tunnel in America, cutting straight through a mountain.

Little Bill was hired as a "shaker," who held a spike in place, while John Henry signed on as a "driver," who hammered the steel drill into the rock to make an opening for blasting powder. Bill had to keep "shaking" the drill free of rock dust, and get it ready for John's next swing. Another man might have been afraid of the power and

speed of John Henry's blows—each driving the drill an inch deeper into solid rock. But Bill knew his partner was keen of eye and always hit the drill straight on the head, so he never blinked once, no matter how fast John drove the steel.

Though the work was hard and the days were hot, John loved to think that his hammering was helping to make a tunnel through which trains would soon roar.

Proud as John Henry was of his work, his boss, Captain Walters, was even prouder of his steel-driving giant. "He's my finest driver," he would boast. "I'd match him against any man."

4

While the work toughened John Henry's arms, his heart was always tender. And the tenderest spot was reserved for Lucy, who worked as a maid on a plantation. She was short to his tall, coffee and cream to his ebony, and appeared cotton-soft compared to his steel-hard muscles. But she was a "steel-driving woman," who came from a family of railroad workers. She could lay down rails second only to John Henry, if she had a mind to.

They would stroll the dusty country lanes in the evening, hand in hand, when their work was done.

"Someday, we're gonna have our own farm near my folks," said John Henry, loving the way Lucy's face crinkled into a happy smile when she heard this.

"When'll that be, John?" she asked.

"When I've had my fill of railroad work," he answered. "And when we've saved up enough to buy a place."

They were married soon afterward. Preacher Henry came all the way from Virginia to perform the wedding. Little Bill was John Henry's best man, and the whole railroad crew turned out. They all chipped in and bought John a new twenty-pound hammer, and gave Lucy a flapjack turner big enough to flip a hotcake the size of a wagon wheel.

John and Lucy set up housekeeping in one of the little wooden shanties that housed all the workers on the Big Bend.

But soon word reached the tunneling crew that the owners of the C&O Railroad were thinking of buying a newly invented steam drill to replace many workers.

The Yankee inventor and several C&O bosses brought the steam drill to the Big Bend for testing. The bosses planned to buy the machine, if it worked as well as its inventor boasted.

John Henry, Little Bill, and the other men looked at the steam drill, and laughed. They called it "the iron monster."

"My machine will drill a hole faster than any *ten* men!" the Yankee challenged.

When the bosses nodded, the crew began to fear they would lose their jobs. John Henry thought about the farm he and Lucy were saving to buy. And he thought about trains roaring through the tunnel that folks would say was dug by a machine, not a good, honest man's work.

John went to Captain Walters and said, "You go to the bosses and you say, 'I've got a man that'll beat that steam drill down. He'll show the world a man is better than that iron monster.' Then you tell 'em, 'And if he does, you gotta keep all the men working until the Big Bend tunnel is finished.' "

The next day, Captain Walters said to the bosses, "I've got a driver—John Henry—who can swing two twenty-pound hammers. I'll match him against your machine, and he'll beat that contraption of yours to a frazzle."

Because the workers were growing angry at the thought of losing their jobs, and the bosses didn't want any trouble, they agreed to a bet. They would hold a thirty-minute contest. If the steam drill could outdrill John Henry, the C&O would buy it and fire the workers. But if John Henry won, they would pay him one hundred dollars, and he and the other men could keep their jobs.

When Lucy heard the news, she rushed over to the tunnel mouth. It was a hot July afternoon, and she was very worried.

"John, even you can't match the speed and power of that iron monster," she said.

"The men are countin' on me," he answered, softly kissing her. "And that hundred dollars means we can buy our farm. Besides, a

man ain't nothin' but a man. I gotta prove that no machine can drill better than a sledgehammer and steel in an honest man's hand.''

Lucy knew that she couldn't keep him from doing what he'd made up his mind to do, so she hugged him all the more tightly.

Then the man-giant and the steam drill lined up side by side, near the end of the tunnel, while a big crowd gathered inside.

The starter dropped his flag.

The contest began.

7

At first, the steam-powered drill pulled steadily ahead.

But this only made John Henry slam his hammer down faster, until the sound of the splitting rock was so loud that some people ran out of the tunnel, thinking the mountain was cracking in half. By the time the contest was halfway over, John Henry's spikes were biting just as deep as the machine's, while the men cheered.

Soon John's twenty-pounders were rising and falling so fast on the steel spikes that Little Bill set down, they were almost invisible. The sweat poured down his face, and he grunted as he strained to lift his hammers.

But though his breath burned like fire in his lungs, John slammed away. He smiled when he saw the steam drill beginning to overheat, and shake, while the Yankee inventor pulled levers and mopped his brow and muttered to himself.

Between breaths, John sang,

Can't she drive 'em!

Can't she drive 'em!

John pulled farther ahead. His muscles were aching and the rock seemed to be growing harder, but this only made him sing louder and pound even more forcefully. Just before Captain Walters yelled, "Time!" the mechanical spike driver shook and wheezed and ground to a halt.

But John Henry could not slow down at first. He drove his spike several inches deeper, before he suddenly fell into the arms of Little Bill. Then the men carried him out of the tunnel.

There, Lucy ran to him, and held his head in her lap, and wiped his face with her handkerchief.

"Lucy, my Lucy," he gasped.

"I'm here, John," she said.

"Did I beat that old steam drill?"

"You did," she said, letting her tears fall like cool rain on his burning face. "No man coulda done better."

"Little Bill," John Henry asked, "where's my hammer?"

Little Bill put John's twenty-pounder in his friend's hand.

"Oh, Lucy, I hear a rollin' and a roarin' in my head, like a locomotive rushin' down the tracks," John said. Then his soul boarded the train only he could see.

When they measured, they found that John Henry had drilled a hole fourteen feet deep, while the steam drill had only reached nine feet.

"He was the best steel-driving man in the whole United States," said Captain Walters. And the railroad workers, whose jobs had been saved by John Henry, agreed as they wept along with Lucy and Little Bill.

But though John Henry died that hot July day, his story has become a part of railroad life and legend. And wherever a train speeds over the tracks, some part of John Henry rides the rails with it.

Old Stormalong: The Deep-Water Sailor

A

lfred Bulltop Stormalong—or Stormy, as he was nicknamed—was the greatest Yankee deep-water sailorman to put out from Cape Cod, in the days of wooden ships and iron men. He was born in a little village on the Maine coast, and when fully grown, he stood twenty-four feet tall.

Stormalong always loved the sea. As a child, he'd play along the seashore, and sometimes swim a hundred miles or more from Maine to Cape Cod, just to roughhouse with the boys there.

He first shipped out as a cabin boy on the *Lady of the Sea*, when he was thirteen and just over six feet tall. Because his daddy—himself a Yankee captain—had taught him, he already knew his way around a ship, from bow to stern and from keel to crow's nest. He could climb the rigging or tie sailor knots with the best old salt.

Shortly after he was promoted to bosun, the ship anchored at sea to ride out a storm. But when the winds died down, and the crew tried to raise anchor, they couldn't lift it. The anchor would give a bit, then sink right back, as though huge hands had pulled it under.

When Stormy added his strength, they were able to haul it close enough to the surface to see that a giant octopus had wrapped half its arms around the anchor, while half were holding on to seaweed and rocks on the bottom.

"Blow me down!" cried the captain. "What'll we do?"

By way of an answer, Stormalong jumped overboard and disappeared beneath the waves. A minute later, the water began to churn, while the *Lady of the Sea*, still tied to the anchor, dipped and bobbed like a float on a fishing line that's hooked a big one. Captain and crew were tossed from side to side, the whole ship creaked and groaned, and all the pots in the kitchen tumbled down on the cook.

Then the water was still. The sailors looked over the rail, shook their heads sadly, and took off their caps out of respect for the bosun who had been everybody's friend.

Suddenly, there was a cry of "Ahoy!" as Stormalong's head appeared. While his mates cheered, he climbed hand over hand up the anchor chain.

"Raise anchor!" he cried, as soon as he planted his feet on deck. This time, the huge mudhook came up without a hitch.

"What about the octopus?" asked the skipper.

"I tied each of his eight tentacles in a different sailor's knot," laughed Stormalong. He counted off on his fingers, "Reef Knot, Half Hitch, Bowline, Sheepshank, Stunner Hitch, Cat's Paw, Becket Bend, and Fisherman's Bend. It'll take him a month of Sundays to untie himself."

Not long after this, the Revolutionary War began. When Stormalong heard that John Paul Jones was enlisting sailors for the first American navy, he went to look at the commander's ship, the *Bon Homme Richard.* He decided, "It's big enough so's it won't cramp my style," and signed on as a sailor.

Stormy had his night of glory in 1779, when the *Bon Homme Richard* joined battle with the *Serapis,* the headship in the King's Navy. The ships closed, firing cannonballs at each other.

"Looks like we're in for a little trouble!" yelled Stormalong, who was at the wheel, when three of the American cannons were blown

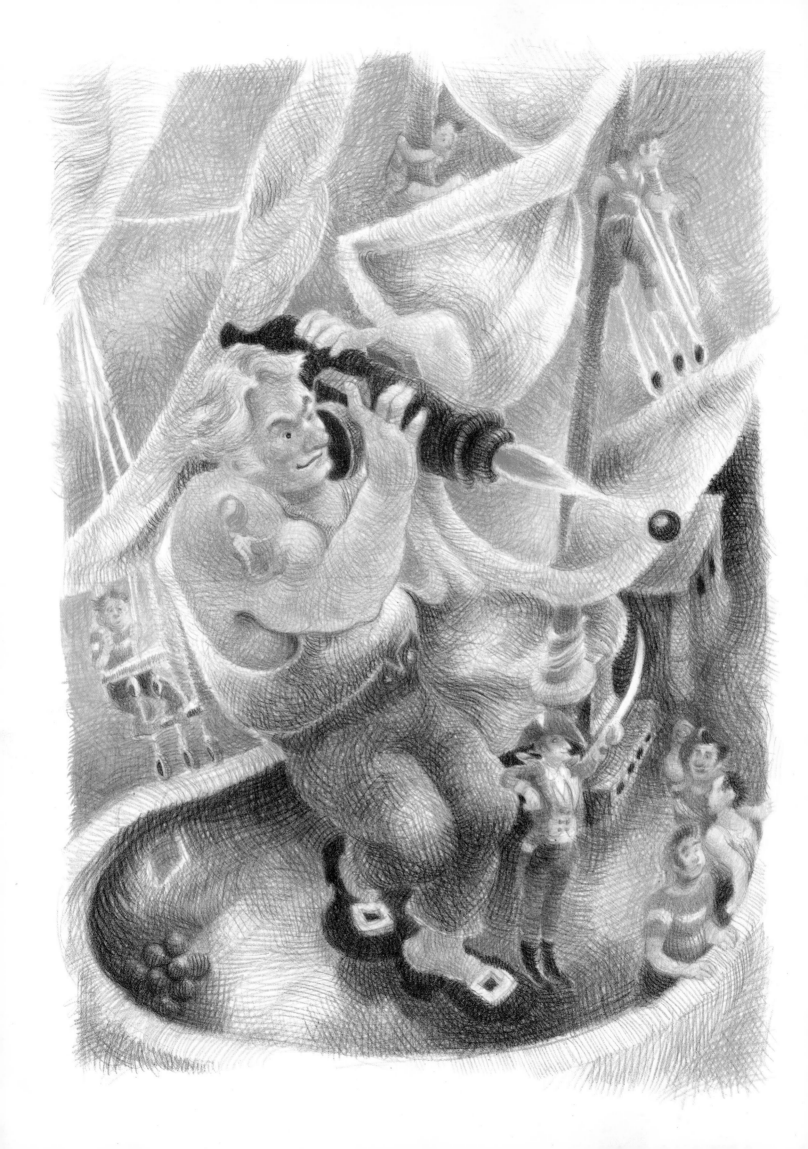

to bits. Then a big hole was opened in their side. Looking over the railing, Stormy reported, "Might be we're sinking, too."

"Are you ready to surrender?" the British captain called across to the Americans.

"Sir, I have not yet begun to fight," John Paul Jones shouted back.

"Heck, we're sort of just getting the hang of it," yelled Stormy, throwing a cannonball with his bare hands that sent the British captain running for cover.

"What do you suggest?" John Paul Jones asked Stormalong above the sounds of battle.

"I say we board them," said Stormy. "I'd feel better about fighting with a deck under me, instead of water."

"Good man! Steer away!" ordered John Paul Jones.

So Stormalong brought around the *Bon Homme Richard*, which was tilting badly, and aimed for the *Serapis*. Cannonballs from the other ship ripped through the sails before the ships collided with a splintering sound.

"Well done, man!" cried John Paul Jones. "Now throw out the grappling hooks, and let's board her."

Faster than the eye could follow, Stormy flung two dozen hooks over the railings of the *Serapis*, pulling the ships together. Then he and John Paul Jones and the rest of the crew, hanging from sails and ropes, swung across onto the enemy deck. There Stormy brought a cannon to his shoulder and fired it the way a man might fire a rifle.

When the fighting was over and the captain of the *Serapis* surrendered, the Americans took possession of the ship. They had to leave the valiant *Bon Homme Richard* to sink.

After the war, John Paul Jones asked Stormy to stay on and serve with him. But Stormalong said, "I'm going to keep watch by the Boston docks, until I find a ship that'll give me a little more room."

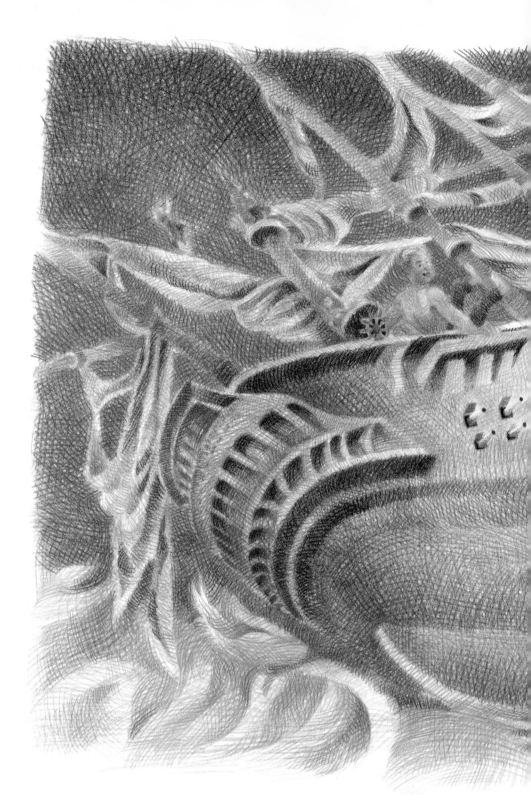

He found his dream ship soon after: the *Albatross*, a giant clipper too large to enter Boston Harbor, dropping anchor outside. Her cargo, from India, China, or Russia, had to be put onto smaller ships that carried the goods to shore.

"Now *this* is a ship for a grown man," Stormalong said happily. And he quickly signed on as a crewman.

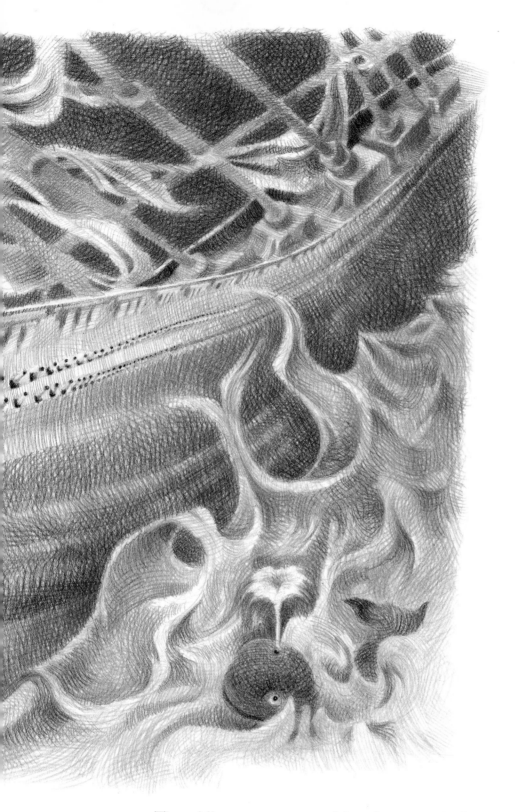

The *Albatross* was so big, the captain kept a stable of horses on deck, so that the men on watch could ride fore to aft. Her masts were so tall that the top parts were on hinges so they would not hit the moon or sun. Men who climbed up to the crow's nest to serve as lookout went up as smooth-faced young men and came down with long gray beards.

It took thirty-four men to turn the wheel. Only Stormalong could handle it by himself.

Usually the *Albatross* was not bothered by bad weather. But one storm was so fierce, the ship was driven every which way. The howling winds and waves would have surely sunk any smaller ship. Through it all, Stormalong kept the wheel, holding the ship to what he thought was the right direction.

When the sun returned, and they could see where they were, they discovered they were in the North Sea, headed for the English Channel. Since the North Sea was not big enough for the *Albatross* to turn around in, they were in danger of getting stuck between the black cliffs at Dover and the French coast.

"Will she make it through?" the captain asked Stormalong.

"I think so," said Stormalong. "But you'd better send all hands over to soap the sides."

The captain shouted orders to the sailors, who climbed over the railings and, hanging from ropes, soaped as they were told.

"Put more on the English side," called Stormy. "Step lively now, or there's gonna be trouble."

The crew kept adding more soap, until there wasn't room enough for a man to squeeze in between the side of the *Albatross* and the British coast.

Then the ship—just barely—squeaked through. But the squeeze was so tight, the ship's sides rubbed up against land on the English side. The soap scraped off, and that is how the cliffs at Dover became white.

In time, Stormalong became captain of the *Albatross*. He'd sit on deck, having a dozen ostrich eggs, each served on a loaf of bread, for breakfast. For supper, he liked a good fish soup served in a Cape Cod boat and hot shark steaks rushed up from the kitchen by ten sailors

pushing wheelbarrows. He would wash this down with a barrel of
whale milk mixed with Maine apple cider, sucked up through a firehose
he used as a straw. When he was finished, he'd stroll the decks,
picking his teeth with a marlinespike.

Then he would sigh happily, and say to the first mate, "It sure
feels good not being cramped for space. A sailor needs a ship that fits
him. When he's got that, he's got everything he needs."

Over the years, his travels took him to Italy, where he once
leaned against the tower of Pisa, which has been tilted ever since. In
Australia, when he bought himself some new clothes and threw away
the old, the fleas that escaped became known as kangaroos.

One day, Old Stormy said to his first mate, "I feel it's time to move on again. Even the *Albatross* is feeling a bit small."

"But there's no bigger ship anywhere," said the mate.

"Not on any earthly sea," Stormy agreed.

Soon after that, he died peacefully in his sleep.

He was mourned by every American sailor. It took ten acres of sailcloth to make his shroud. The *Albatross*, taking him for burial at sea, was followed by a line of ghost ships, including the valiant *Bon Homme Richard* and many others that had been sunk in battle or wrecked by storms.

Behind them, Father Neptune led a double line of seahorses ridden by weeping mermaids.

Alfred Bulltop Stormalong was lowered into the sea on silver chains, to rest forever in the ocean that was his first and lasting love.

But he lives on, in the stories about him that are shared by deep-water sailors everywhere.

Slue-Foot
Sue
and Pecos
Bill

One hot Texas afternoon, Slue-Foot Sue decided to walk to the Rio Grande. She had finished roofing the new henhouse, and felt the need for a river breeze and a catfish ride.

Sue was a big, brawny girl who could do the work of ten men. She had spent the morning branding cattle, shoeing horses, and building a hencoop. Now she stopped by one of the sheds and took out a long leather

strap that was neatly coiled up. With this over her shoulder, she hurried on to the river's edge.

There she put her two little fingers between her lips and whistled so loud that people in the next state reached for teakettles that weren't even on the fire.

In answer, a catfish bigger than any whale swam up to the bank. It waited in the shallows, twitching its whiskers, while Sue put the leather strap around the fish's middle. Then, with a cry of "Yippy yippy ay!" she and the catfish plunged into the river. They raced against the current, with Sue holding on to the strap like a bareback rider. Her long, copper-colored hair flowed out behind her.

"YEE-HAW!" yelled Sue as they rounded a bend in the river.

" 'YEE-HAW,' yourself!" called a voice from above. Looking up, she saw a near-giant of a cowboy on the finest-looking horse she had ever seen. Sue waved her bonnet at him and cried, "Howdy!"

He waved back, and she steered her catfish into a cove.

When both had dismounted, the cowboy took off his hat and introduced himself. "Name's Pecos Bill," he said, giving his mustache a twist. "This here's my horse, Widow Maker." He gave the horse a pat on the flank.

"My name's Slue-Foot Sue," she said. "I'm called that because of this trick foot of mine."

She showed him how her right foot turned in toward the left.

"You're already pretty as bluebonnets on a hill," said Pecos. "Seems that only makes you more special." Then he turned red as a tomato, and Sue could see that he had fallen for her. That was all right by her, since she had fallen for him, too.

Sue unfastened the strap from around the catfish and sent it out into the river with a gentle slap.

"You're turnin' him loose?" asked Bill.

"He comes anytime I whistle," said Sue, tossing her coppery hair.

"Well, it sure was nice makin' your acquaintance, but I've got to be headin' home now."

"Can I walk you there?" asked Pecos, and Sue agreed.

As they strolled along, with Widow Maker following, Pecos told Sue how he had been raised by coyotes, tamed a cyclone, built the Perpetual Motion Ranch on Pinnacle Mountain, and lots more.

"Had a few adventures myself," said Sue. "Remember the big rain last winter?"

"That rain was a gully-washer and fence-lifter, all right," agreed Pecos with a shake of his head.

"My daddy's ranch would've been flooded out for sure," said Sue, "if I hadn't whistled up some of my big ol' catfish to make a dam around the ranch and keep the water out. But the worst was, the barn blew down, and I had to keep the cows and horses under my slicker until the rain let up."

"You're some gal," said Pecos.

So they walked and talked and somehow, though it was only a short distance to Sue's house, they didn't reach there until nearly sundown.

Sue introduced Pecos to her mother and father, who were polite, but didn't make him feel very welcome. They sat him in a room filled with spindly-shanked furniture and fancy things from back east, and only wanted to talk about the weather. But after saying that it was "Mighty hot" and "Don't look much like rain," Pecos ran out of things to say.

It got pretty quiet in the room then, until Sue's grandmother burst in. She shook Pecos's hand as if she were working a pump handle.

"You got a mighty fine grip," Pecos said, wiggling his fingers to be sure they were still working.

"You bet," she said. "I'm a rip-tail roarer for sure. I can wade the Mississippi without getting wet, outholler a mountain lion, and dance

down any fellow in Arkansas or Texas. And my granddaughter's just like me," she said with a wink at Sue.

Sue laughed, but her mother and father sat stiff and pale.

"I've gotta be gettin' back to my own place," said Pecos, "but . . . I'd sure like to visit you again, if it's all right."

"I'd like that," Sue said, blushing prettily.

"Gal knows a good thing when she sees it," said Sue's grandmother, winking at Pecos this time.

So Pecos would ride over to Sue's every evening from the Perpetual Motion Ranch, and his visiting very quickly turned to courting. He'd call her "My Little Coyote," and he'd bring his banjo to play her songs he'd written just for her.

He would do anything for his ladylove—almost.

Sue often asked, "Will you let me ride Widow Maker?"

But he would shake his head. "The only other person, 'cept me, who tried it was Curley Joe. Widow Maker tossed him onto the top of Pike's Peak. Since then, I don't let anyone ride my horse but me."

Sue asked again and again, but his answer was always the same.

Well, it wasn't long before Pecos asked Sue to be his bride, and she said yes, and the two of them were happy as pigs in a peanut patch. Pecos gave her his rattlesnake whip as an engagement present.

"I want a fancy weddin'," Sue told her mama and papa. So her bridal gown was sent out from St. Louis, and with it came a brand-new bustle, made of the finest steel.

Sue's grandma looked at the bustle and said, "I ain't never seen such foolishness as that."

But when Sue saw herself all dressed up in a looking glass, she was pleased, and knew Pecos would be, too.

On their wedding day, when Sue climbed down from her daddy's carriage at the Perpetual Motion Ranch, she looked so grand that Pecos Bill felt he'd burst with pride, while Alkali Ike, Cheyenne Charley, and all his men clapped and hooted. This made Sue whoop with pleasure, while her father and mother just shook their heads.

"Let's get 'em hitched up, Rev'rend," said Sue's grandmother, "so we can get to the eatin' and dancin' part." Then she pounded the preacher so good-naturedly on the back that the poor man was sent spinning into a haystack and had to be rescued by Pecos.

When they were married, Sue whispered, "Promise me one thing, Bill."

"Just ask me, darlin'," he answered. "I promise."

"I want to ride Widow Maker," she said, "and a promise is a promise."

So he unhappily went and got Widow Maker.

"Look here," said Pecos to his horse, "Sue's my bouncin' bride, and you're gonna treat her kind 'n' gentle, aren't you?"

Widow Maker lowered his head and wouldn't look at Pecos. The uneasy feeling in Pecos grew.

But over came Sue, and Pecos helped his bride to mount.

What happened next depends on who is telling the story. Some claim that Widow Maker had it in for the bride all along. Others say it was Sue's slue foot that turned in and tickled the horse in the ribs.

Whatever the cause, no one can argue the effect: Widow Maker bucked and before Pecos could cry "Whoa!" the horse sent poor Sue into the sky. Sue sailed over the mountains, flying so high that she had to duck her head to keep from hitting the moon.

When she'd gone as high as she could, and started back down to earth, she saw Pecos holding out his arms to catch her.

But just when she felt safe, the wind caught hold of her fancy bustle and sent her in another direction, so that she hit the side of a distant mountain. The bustle acted like a big spring and she bounced sky-high.

Well, poor Sue kept on bouncing between the earth and the moon all day, while Bill ran every which way, trying to catch her. Sue's folks

fainted dead away on her first bounce, but her grandma only said, "I *knew* that thing was trouble."

"SAVE ME!" Sue cried. She was getting sore and so hungry that she started breaking off bits of the moon's green cheese every time she passed it, so that the moon went from full to crescent in no time.

When she'd lost count of how many times she'd bounced, Sue suddenly got an idea. She tried signaling Pecos to lasso her by circling her arm.

But Pecos thought she was bravely waving to him. "That's a gal with real spunk," he said and waved back, and so did all the other cowboys. The faster Sue circled her arm, the more cheering and waving came from Pecos Bill and his men. "No, no, no!" shouted Sue, who was getting angry and hoarse from all her yelling. The wind and the bustle kept her going in as many different directions as popcorn on a hot griddle.

Finally, Sue's grandma, who had been making bets with Alkali Ike and Cheyenne Charley about where Sue would land each time (and winning), figured out what her granddaughter was signaling. She yelled to Pecos, "Lasso the child!"

Pecos ran for his rope, shook out the noose, and whirled it around his head in ever growing circles, faster and faster. Then—*zip!*—he let it fly, his eyes glued to his bride. The rope shot out true as an arrow; the noose slipped neatly over Sue's shoulders and tightened around her waist.

So he pulled her in. He thought Sue would be happy, but she was tired and angry and feeling foolish. She gathered up her mother and father and grandmother, and drove off in the carriage, leaving Pecos Bill and his crew staring after them.

When the family got back to the ranch, Sue's mama and papa decided they'd had enough of the wild life and wanted to move back east. Sue, who was still mad as a hornet, decided to go with them.

When they reached the banks of the Mississippi River, Sue's grandmother asked her, "How much sense you got, girl?"

"Enough to know beans from buzzard's tails," Sue answered.

"Enough to know when you're makin' a dilly of a mistake?"

"Sure enough!" cried Sue, hugging the old woman. Then, while her mother and father stared in disbelief, Sue whistled up the biggest Mississippi catfish, threw a strap around it, and set off for New Orleans and the Gulf of Mexico.

Where the freshwater river met the saltwater sea, she changed mounts, heading for Texas on the back of a whale.

When she reached Texas, she bought herself a raring, tearing, snorting horse, and set out for the Perpetual Motion Ranch.

There Alkali Ike told her, "Bill couldn't stay on the ranch without you. He took off into the mountains, and we haven't seen hide nor hair o' him since."

Sue quickly picked up Pecos Bill's trail into the hills. After a day and a night tracking him, she found Pecos and Widow Maker trapped in a box canyon by an army of the biggest, meanest-looking coyotes she'd ever seen. Even if Pecos had been in good spirits, the coyotes would have been something to reckon with. But the spirit had gone out of him when Sue left.

The old Pecos returned fast enough when he saw Sue come charging down into the canyon, cracking the rattlesnake whip he had given her. Then Pecos fired his gun into the air, and the two of them chased the coyote army all the way into the badlands.

After that, they lived for a time on a ranch they built just west of the Pecos River. But one day Sue turned to Pecos and said, "The West is gettin' too tame for the likes o' me."

"I could use a little more excitement myself," Pecos agreed.

So they set off together in search of adventure, to the Argentine and Australia and Africa and all sorts of places.

And the word is, they're traveling to this day.

Strap Buckner: The Texas Fighter

ne of the greatest heroes of Texas was Strap Buckner. He was called Strap because he was such a strapping big fellow. He was the size of a grizzly bear, and as strong as ten wildcats. His face was ruddy and freckled; his hair was red as fire and bushy as the mane of an African lion.

He was a kind and generous man at heart, but his strength was his pride. And his downfall was his love of fighting. He would wade into the middle of any fight already underway—or start one if things were too quiet. When the fight was over, he was always the last man standing. Then he would help those he had knocked down to their feet in a friendly manner, thank them politely for their time, and say he was sorry for any broken bones or bruises he had caused.

He was often heard to say, however, "The folks in this town can't give me a fair fight. Where's the fun in that?"

About this time, a huge black bull named Noche, which is Spanish for "Night," appeared near town. The animal tossed men with a flick of his horns, and people were afraid to go out of doors.

"Now *here's* a *real* contest for me!" Strap cried. He marched out to face the wild bull, while the townsfolk watched from doors and windows.

Strap threw a red blanket over his shoulder like a bullfighter. When Noche saw him, his tail shot up like a flagpole, then began shifting back and forth. The bull snorted and pawed the ground and roared loud enough to rattle teacups and teeth.

But Strap just grinned and began to do the same as Noche. He pawed the ground with his boot, and he roared even louder than the bull.

Noche, angry at being made fun of, charged the man like a train that had jumped its tracks. But Strap stood his ground. At the last minute, he swung his fist and hit the bull's forehead, making a sound like a thunderclap.

The bull stood frozen in place for a minute, then he staggered back and dropped down with a thud. When he could climb to his feet again, he turned tail and raced away—nor was he ever seen in those parts again.

The townsfolk crowded around Strap and called him a hero. But he just rubbed his knuckles and said, "That there was a good *warm-up,* but I still haven't found anyone who can give me a *real fight.*"

Still eager to meet such a match, he decided to move on. Taking his big iron club in his right hand and tossing a bundle of blankets and clothes over his left shoulder, he set out to find someone who could truly test his strength.

Strap traveled west, over the plains, until he came to a small trading post run by Bob Turket and Bill Smotherall. They traded beads and blankets and other things to the Indians for hides and furs.

These two traders were good fighters themselves, and fought with each other when there was no one else around. When Strap met them, Bob took a punch at him, then Bill did. With a whoop of pleasure, Strap knocked them both down, one-two. Then he kindly helped them to their feet, and they all shook hands and became fast friends.

Bob and Bill introduced him to the chief of the Indian tribe living nearby. Right away, Strap knocked the chief down, along with all his Indian braves. Then Strap pulled the chief back to his feet, shook his hand, and said, "Pleased to meet you. Sorry, I didn't catch the name."

"I am Chief Tuleahcahoma," the great warrior said, brushing himself off.

"That's a mouthful for certain," said Strap. "I'll just call you 'Chief.'"

The Indian agreed to this. He and his people were great fighters themselves, and were so impressed with Strap's strength, they made him a member of the tribe.

"We will call you 'Red Son of Blue Thunder,'" said Chief, "because you have red hair and you strike a blow that sounds like thunder."

Then the great chief presented him with a gray horse, the largest and swiftest horse the tribe owned.

Strap was so pleased with his new friends, he decided to settle down. Only one thing made him unhappy: he still had not found anyone who could match him in a fight.

Strap built himself a fine cabin. In the afternoons, he would go walking and knock down just about everyone he met. And for a time, he was content.

One day, however, he rode his swift gray horse to the trading post, his long red hair flying out behind him like a comet's tail. There he found Chief, Bob Turket, and Bill Smotherall playing cards.

They invited Strap to join in the game, but the cards were against him. In anger, he slammed them down and sent his three friends flying.

"Something bothering you, Strap?" asked Bill, rubbing his jaw.

"Aw, I'm getting the fidgets," Strap said. "I just can't be happy until I fight someone who can give me a run for my money!"

Then he strode to the door of the trading post, and roared in a voice that was heard throughout the hills and forests on all sides, "Here I stand, Strap Buckner, the fightingest, bravest rip-roarer that ever lived. Where is the man who can knock me down?

"If there's someone who dares, let him step forth. I'll bet my gray horse I can beat him. Man, beast, or the devil himself! I'll fight you!"

At these words, a booming came from the forests and hills all around. The ground began to shake, so that Bob Turket and Bill Smotherall and Chief hung on to each other, pale and frightened.

A loud voice, like a huge tree trunk breaking in half, roared back, "Strap Buckner, you'll have your fight."

Then all was quiet.

Chief looked at Strap, shook his head, and left.

"Strap," said Bob Turket weakly, "maybe you shouldn't boast so loud."

But Strap just laughed at this. His eyes burned with the fire of a man about to have his wish fulfilled. He rubbed his hands eagerly, saying, "I've got the fight I want coming, boys!" And he clapped Bob and Bill on their backs so heartily he felled them both.

Then he leapt onto the saddle of his gray horse and rode away. But his friends saw a strange creature like a red monkey appear on the back of the horse. It turned and thumbed its nose at them, then disappeared in a puff of blue smoke, though Strap didn't notice this.

It was late in the evening when Strap reached his cabin and climbed down from his horse. Thunder rolled over the hills, while purple lightning lit the clouds. Inside his cabin, Strap ate a big dinner of hoecake and fried bacon with gusto, while the storm rattled his windows.

Suddenly, Strap heard a laugh.

Turning, he saw a strange little figure, black as his iron frying pan, with eyes like two live coals, dancing near the fireplace. It was shaped like a man, but was only two feet high. With a clawed hand, it thumbed a nose hooked like an eagle's beak at Strap. As it danced among the flames, a long tail with a sharp point snapped in the air behind it.

"Who the devil are *you?*" Strap cried, grabbing his iron club.

"Skin for skin," piped the figure. "Skin for skin."

"What do you want?" Strap asked.

But the figure just danced out into the middle of the floor. Then it grew taller, until its head was at Strap's chest. "Skin for skin," it said again.

" 'Skin for skin?' What does that mean?" Strap wondered.

But the creature grew again, and now its glowing red eyes were as high as Strap's own. "You challenged the devil to a fight, and I'm here to take up your challenge. But, instead of betting your horse, the

bet I have in mind is this: my skin for yours. Will you accept? You'll find no better match anywhere on the earth or under it. Follow me, if you dare." And the devil stepped outside into the storm.

"Now, *here's* the contest for me!" Strap shouted, so eager for a good fight, and so proud of his strength, he didn't give a thought to what he was risking.

Taking his iron club in his right hand, Strap followed the devil, who led him through the howling wind to a circle of oaks on the top of a nearby hill. The green grass inside made a perfect ring for the devil and Strap to fight each other.

Then, roaring with laughter, the devil suddenly began to grow and grow until he was one hundred and ninety feet tall and eighty feet across at the shoulders. His forked tail whipped back and forth, cutting the tops off the tallest oaks.

"This is no fair fight," complained Strap. "All bets are off."

The devil looked down and said in a voice that shook the trees more than the storm, "I don't like cold iron. Put down your weapon, and I'll resume a height more to your liking."

Strap tossed aside his iron club. At the same moment, the devil started shrinking until he was exactly Strap's size. Both raised their fists like boxers. They circled each other, punching and ducking, dancing close and jumping back.

Blow after blow connected. First one and then the other was knocked down. But the devil bounced back more quickly, because he wound his tail into a spring. Each time, Strap would whoop with delight to have found a fighter who could go the distance.

Round by round, they went at it—lit by lightning and covered with mud. First one and then the other would get in a lucky blow. But they were such a good match, neither got the best of the other for a while. The mountains around them rang with the sounds of their contest.

Bob Turket and Bill Smotherall on the porch of their trading post, and Chief and his people in their village, watched the ring of oak trees shudder and shake. None of them dared to go see what was happening.

But, he was so eager for a good fight, Strap forgot that a fight with the devil can never really be a fair match. And Strap Buckner, for all his strength, was still a man; and little by little, he became so tired out that his eyes grew heavy and he couldn't raise his arms.

Then the devil threw a final punch, and felled Strap as cleanly as the man had once dropped the bull Noche in his tracks. Now the devil cried, "Skin for skin!" and reached down for the fallen man.

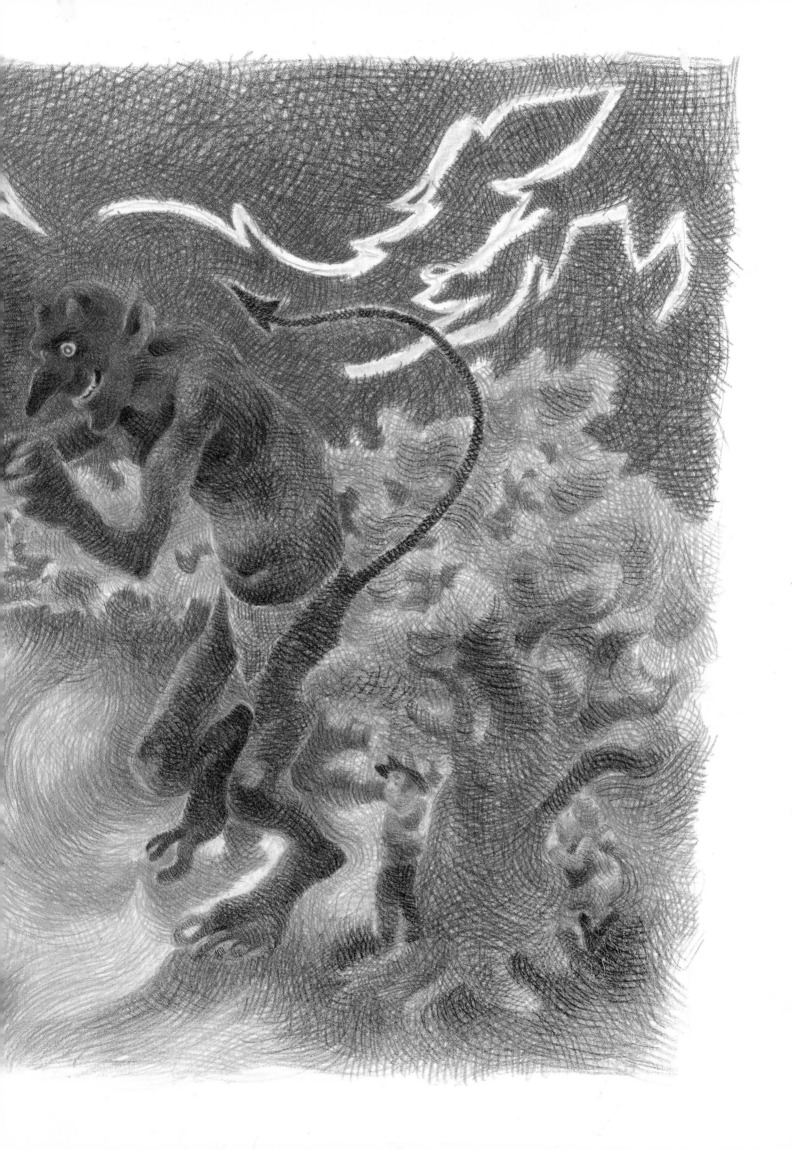

In the morning, Bob and Bill and Chief and his warriors went to where the fateful match had taken place. The ground had been torn away down to the bare rock, and in the rock were the marks of Strap's boots and the devil's hooves. Afterward, nothing would ever grow there.

Nor was Strap Buckner ever seen in those parts again. But, on stormy nights, when the wind howls and the thunder roars, a huge blue flame will suddenly shoot across the black clouds, turning the landscape blue. And, people say, when you look at that fiery bridge, you'll see galloping across it a great gray horse, ridden by something that looks like a huge red monkey. Behind the creature sits a giant of a man, whose long red hair flies out behind him like the tail of a comet.

Paul Bunyan and Babe the Blue Ox

aul Bunyan, the greatest logger of all time, the giant who pretty much invented the lumber industry, was born and raised in Maine. He had logged off the better part of that state before he turned twenty. After that he did some work in Canada, before he turned up in Michigan. He became boss of a camp on the Big Onion River, where he would cut down so much timber in a day that three hundred mule drivers would have to work day and night to haul his logs to the river. He headed a campful of mighty men, including French Canadians, Swedes, Irishmen, Scots, and any other logger who could give a good account of himself.

But his truest companion was Babe the Blue Ox.

There are different stories of how the two met. One story is that Paul found Babe during the Winter of the Blue Snow.

On that special morning, Paul woke just before dawn, broke up the ice on a little lake nearby and washed his face, parted his hair with a hand ax, and combed his beard with a crosscut saw. Then he went out looking for a stand of trees to cut down, walking through the blue snow that filled the woods. Suddenly he heard bellowing from the direction of the frozen river. There he discovered a young ox, already bigger than a full-grown steer, splashing in the water where the ice had given way under it.

"Hold on!" cried the softhearted logger. Kneeling down on the snowy bank, he fished out the soggy calf. The poor thing had been white when he had fallen in, but had turned bright blue from the cold before Paul pulled him out of the icy river.

Paul carried the creature back to camp through a blue blizzard, saying, "There, there, poor little baby." When they reached Big Onion Camp, Paul built a barn for the ox he had already begun to call "Babe." Then he searched the mountains around for moose moss to make soup for the calf.

As it turned out, when Babe was spoon-fed love and soup, he grew so fast, that the next morning, Paul found the barn he had built sitting on the ox's back. Then Paul put his hands on his hips and said with a smile, "You're sure gonna be something t' reckon with." Then he scratched at his beard thoughtfully, and added, "You have so much power, it shouldn't be wasted. When you're grown up, I'll find you some useful work."

Babe made a soft, chuckling sound, as if to say, "That's fine with me."

Paul kept on feeding Babe, and pretty soon the animal was up to full size, measuring forty-two ax handles between the eyes. An ordinary

person standing at Babe's head or tail would have to use a telescope to see what was happening at the other end.

Some people say that Paul dug the Great Lakes so that Babe would always have fresh water. A lot of the smaller lakes in Wisconsin and Minnesota, they add, are simply Babe's hoofprints filled with water.

Babe's shoes were made by the blacksmith Ole Olsen, who sank to his knees in solid rock the first time he tried to carry one.

At first there was a lot of grumbling, because Paul put part of his crew to work bringing in enough hay to feed Babe. "That critter's a waste of hay and time," some men said.

The matter was settled by Johnny Inkslinger, Paul's bookkeeper. He used a special fountain pen that was eighteen feet long and connected by a three-foot hose to thirty-eight barrels of ink on the shelf over his desk. Always looking for a way to save a penny, Johnny once saved nine barrels of ink over a winter by not crossing his t's or dotting his i's. He pointed out, "Babe really *saves* us money. He can haul the lumber in one trip that we needed three hundred mule drivers for. Thanks to him, we make more money. That means your paychecks are bigger."

This fact—if not the milk of human kindness—quickly made the blue ox popular with the loggers.

Babe, who could haul anything, was a great worker who could drag 640 acres of timberland to the river at one time—all in one piece. There, Paul's crew chopped down the trees, then the blue ox hauled the cleared land back into place.

Paul would also use the blue ox in plenty of other ways. Once, when one of Paul's men sent the wrong lumber down the Mississippi to New Orleans, Paul was faced with the problem of getting the lumber back upstream. What would have seemed impossible to anyone else

just needed a little thinking on Paul's part. He simply fed Babe an extra-big salt ration, then led him to the Mississippi to drink. Babe was so thirsty, he drained the river dry, sucking the water upstream, so that the logs came back faster than they had gone down.

Babe was a fine pet. When he was happy, he would chortle and roll his big blue eyes and stick out his tongue to lick Paul behind the ear or on the back of the neck. This would always send the giant logger into roars of laughter that made folks miles away think thunder was rolling down the mountains.

But Babe loved to play jokes on Paul's crew, and this could make the men angry. He would sometimes go to the lake from which the men got water, and drink it dry in a single swallow. Then the men would have to go thirsty and dirty until the lake filled up again. Once he lay down in the river and dammed it up, not moving until Paul drew him away with a sandwich made of two giant flapjacks with a filling of clover hay.

But even with all of his joking, Babe helped Paul to keep the money rolling in. Paul added more and more men to his crew, building bunkhouses so long that it took three days to walk from one end to the other. To keep his men well fed and happy, Paul hired the best camp cooks around, including Hot Biscuit Slim, Joe Muffinton, Sourdough Sam, Pea Soup Shorty, and Cream Puff Fatty, who made desserts.

At Round River Camp, Paul built a cooking stove so big that it took three hundred cooks standing shoulder to shoulder to keep it going, and a special crew just to supply firewood. When it was time to make flapjacks, a griddle would be lowered onto the stove, and this was greased by the kitchen workers skating along with bacon slabs tied to their feet.

Meals were served by men on roller skates, who raced up and down the long tables Paul had built.

When they were ready to move on to the next camp in North Dakota, Paul got the bright idea of tying all the camp buildings together, with the cookhouse in the lead, and having Babe haul the camp to Red River.

When he yelled, "Gee! Haw! Yay!" Babe pulled the camp over mountains and plains, while the loggers leaned out the cabin windows, waving to anyone they happened to see—though, for the most part, only the wild creatures of the woods saw them pass.

One winter Paul logged off North Dakota with the Seven Axemen, his finest lumberjacks. Stories about the height and weight of the Seven Axemen are different, but people say that they used four-foot logs as toothpicks. When they got working along with Paul, their axes often flew so fast, they sometimes came close to setting fire to the forests.

In the Dakotas, they all got carried away and logged off the whole of the state, until there wasn't much left but bushes. Looking around and feeling a little bad, Paul said, "I think maybe we shoulda stopped a while back."

Sitting on a big stump, Babe beside him, Paul looked out over the sorry wasteland he had helped make. To Babe he said, "I won't let this happen again. It isn't good for the land. And there's nothing left for an honest logger to make a living from."

True to his spirit of making the best of the worst, Paul got up, took a big hammer, and pounded down the stumps into the ground. He turned the Dakotas into smooth, rolling plains that became fine farmland.

But Paul was never able to cross the Dakotas without thinking of the great forests that had disappeared under his ax.

When Paul and his men returned to the North Woods, they found that pine trees, loggers, and a certain blue ox were not the only things that came big-sized there. They were attacked by giant mosquitoes that had to be fought off with pikes and axes. When they tried to escape into a cabin, these monsters would tear off the roof or chew through the log walls.

Paul decided to fight fire with fire, so he sent Sourdough Sam back to Maine for some of the giant bees Paul remembered from his boyhood. Sourdough had to bring the insects back on foot, with their wings tied, because they could not be controlled if they were allowed to fly. He collected their stingers, gave them boots, and marched them two by two to Paul's camp.

But when Paul let the bees go, thinking they would chase away the mosquitoes, he found he had planned wrong. The bees and mosquitoes intermarried, producing offspring with stingers in front and behind, and they got Paul's men coming and going.

Paul got rid of them by sending ships full of sugar and molasses out to the middle of Lake Superior. The insects, who had a bee-like hunger for sweets, swarmed over the ships, eating so much sugar they could not fly, and they drowned trying to get back to shore.

The following year, Paul decided to try his luck among the tall trees of Oregon and Washington, on the Pacific Coast. Since both he and the blue ox were getting a little on in years, Paul bought several thousand oxen to help Babe with the hauling. This worked out fine for several weeks, until tragedy struck.

On the fateful day, one of Paul's crew tied all the oxen together, with Babe in the lead, to haul lumber to the ocean. All went fine until they reached a deep valley. Babe, marching along in front, started up the far side of the valley before the rest of the team had finished coming down. As a result, all the normal-sized oxen were quickly and fatally strung across the valley like laundry drying on a clothesline.

By the time Paul discovered what had happened, there was not much to do but tell the men back at camp that there would be plenty of beef for breakfast, lunch, and dinner.

After that, Babe continued to do the hauling alone. But Paul could see the blue ox was slowing down a bit. And, to tell the truth, he felt himself slowing down some.

To Babe, he said, "All these logging trucks and chain saws and sawmills full of fancy gadgets are making me feel a little useless— even if I invented half the stuff myself."

Babe made a soft sound as if to say, "I agree."

Not long after, they took themselves up to Alaska, where they enjoyed some old-fashioned logging. When they had had their fill of the Arctic, they came back. In a deep woods—in Oregon or Minnesota or Maine, depending on who tells the story—Paul built a cabin for himself and a barn for Babe.

There he keeps two big iron kettles bubbling all the time: one full of pea soup for himself, and one full of moose moss soup for Babe.

In the evenings, Paul sits on his porch and Babe rests nearby, and they listen to the trees growing, which is a joy they had never shared before. And that green, growing power fills them so that they know they will be around as long as a single tree endures.